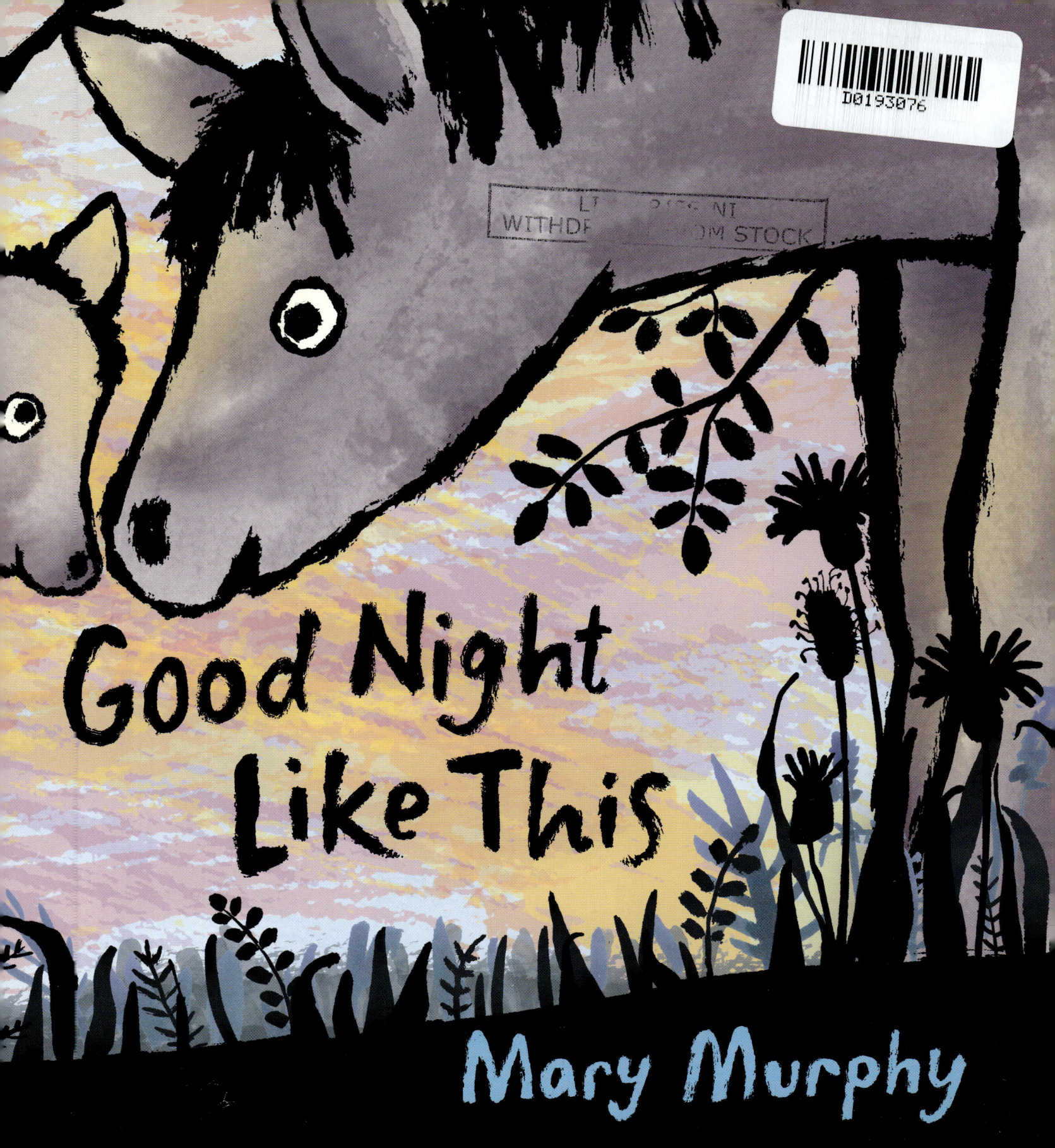

Good Night Like This

Mary Murphy

Yawny
and dozy,
twitchy
and cosy.

Good night,
rabbits,
sleep tight...

Flitty and shiny,
flashy and
tiny.

Good night,
fireflies,
sleep tight...

like
this.

Quiet and strong,
all winter long.

Good night,
bears,
sleep tight...

Tickly
and feathery,
in any old
weathery.

Good night,
ducks,
sleep tight...

Snorey
and furry,
stretchy
and purry.
Good night, cats,
sleep tight...

Swoosh, swish, make a bedtime wish.

Good night, mice, sleep tight…

like
this.

Look! Everyone's tucked up
in bed — now it's your turn,
you sleepyhead.

So, good night,
you,
sleep tight...

Other books by Mary Murphy:

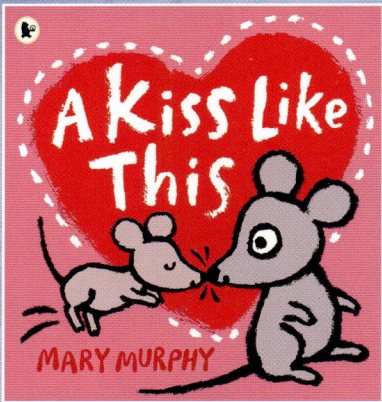

978-1-4063-5994-7

978-1-4063-4538-4

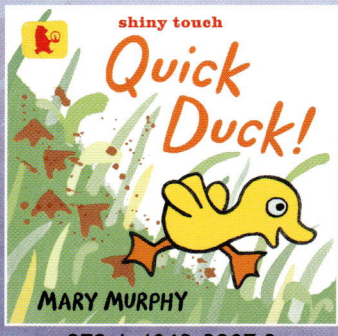

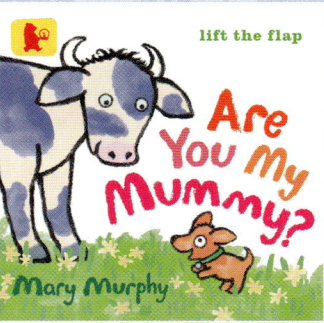

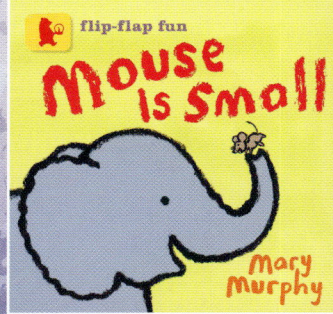

978-1-4063-3908-6

978-1-4063-3907-9

978-1-4063-5378-5

978-1-4063-4828-6

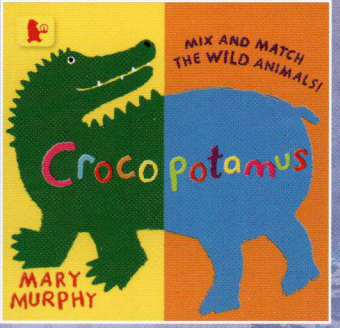

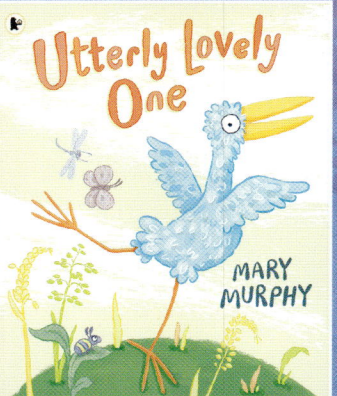

978-1-4063-5789-9

978-1-4063-3774-7

Available from all good booksellers

www.walker.co.uk